THE
SAND WITCH

ReadZone Books Limited

www.ReadZoneBooks.com

© in this edition 2015 ReadZone Books Limited

This print edition published in cooperation with Fiction Express, who first published this title in weekly instalments as an interactive e-book.

Fiction Express
First Floor Office, 2 College Street,
Ludlow, Shropshire SY8 1AN
www.fictionexpress.co.uk

Find out more about Fiction Express on pages 85–86.

Design: Laura Durman & Keith Williams
Cover Image: Shutterstock Images

© in the text 2015 Tommy Donbavand
The moral right of the author has been asserted.

ISBN 978-1-783-22544-6

Printed in Malta by Melita Press.

THE
SAND WITCH

TOMMY DONBAVAND

What do other readers think?

Here are some comments left on the Fiction Express blog about this book:

"I love this book. It is so cool it is terrifying."
Sonia, student, Birmingham

*"I love the suspense when you read it.
I was on the edge of my seat reading it!"*
Missymoo, student, Bradford

*"I am extremely amazed by this fabulous story.
I would definitely give you FIVE STARS! I am looking
forward to reading more."*
Peterkin, student, Telford

"I love The Sand Witch *because it's… scary…
and [there's] a lot of action and it makes me laugh."*
Myhra Y, student, Birmingham

*"The Sand Witch is getting better and better.
I got excited and started reading it straight away!
I love your books soo much."*
Kiera W, student, London

Contents

For Sue and Bryan,

and those long days on the beaches of North Wales.

Chapter 1

A Day at the Beach

The crab's claw burst up out of the sand. Razor sharp pincers snapped together in the warm summer breeze, and then the rest of the creature pushed its way out into the sunlight. Bulging, red-veined eyes blinked in the harsh glare, flicking left and right as the hungry animal sought out its next meal. It could taste the salt in the sea air, but there had to be something more satisfying to eat....

And then it spotted the children.

The crab scuttled sideways towards the youngsters, any sound its feet made as it darted over the sand masked by the crashing waves of the sea. The children had no idea what was coming. Reaching its target, the crab opened a claw and lunged for its victim, hissing with delight.

"Ow!" cried Ella Reid, grabbing her toe and rubbing at the spot where the miniature crab had nipped her. "That stung a bit!" She carefully plucked the animal from the sand and dropped it into a bright yellow bucket at her side.

"Mikey!" she said, calling to her younger brother. "Come and have a look at this little fella."

Mikey abandoned the hole he was digging and hurried over to sit beside his sister. He cautiously peered inside the bucket to find the crab scurrying from one corner to another.

"He's tiny!" said Mikey. "What are we going to do with him?

"Give me a minute to put my flip flops back on, then we'll take him over to the rock pools and release him."

An exaggerated sigh came from behind her.

"What's wrong now?" she asked.

Chris – Ella's twin brother – slumped back on the soft sand and groaned. "Rock pools?" he said. "Is that really the most exciting thing you can think of to do?"

"It'll be fun!" said Ella.

"It'll be boring!" retorted Chris. "How long have Mum and Dad been gone now?"

Ella checked her watch. "Sixteen minutes."

"And when will they be back?"

"Well," said Ella with a smile. "Their boat trip lasts for an hour and a half, so you work it out."

Chris sat up, the breeze ruffling his mop of blonde hair. He began to count on his fingers, lips moving with every number. "But that's... that's AGES until they get back! And we have to look after Mikey all that time!"

Ella brushed her own blonde hair from her eyes. "You don't have to look after anyone," said Ella. "Go back to the cottage if you like. I'll stay here and play with Mikey."

Chris turned to glance up at the picturesque holiday cottage standing at the top of the beach, trails of thick, green ivy climbing up its rough stone walls. The family had been lucky to find such a beautiful holiday home, and were delighted to discover that it sat just metres away from a secluded bay. More often than not, there were only one or two families spending time on the sand. Much better than the crowded beach they'd visited the year before.

"I don't want to go to the cottage," said Chris. "There's nothing to do in there either. No DVD player. No games console. And only five TV channels. I want to go to the arcade in town and play 'Alien Blasters'!"

"Mum said you couldn't go to the arcade until she and Dad got back," said Ella. "So, you'll either have to stay here or go back to the cottage."

"The cottage is boring!"

Ella rolled her eyes. "You think everything is boring."

"No," countered Chris. "I think this holiday is boring." He scooped up a handful of sand and let the golden grains run through his fingertips. "How long is it until Mum and Dad are back now?"

It was Ella's turn to sigh. "About three minutes less than the last time you asked me!" She jumped to her feet. "Come on Mikey – let's go and take the little crab back home."

Chris shielded his eyes against the sun and watched as Ella took the toddler's hand and, together, they ambled off towards a couple of shallow pools at the nearest end of the bay. Seagulls cried out as they circled lazily in the air above them.

Chris snatched up Mikey's plastic spade and began to stab at the sand beside him.

"The beach is boring as well!" he muttered to himself. "And it smells of seaweed!"

"Yes!" agreed a sharp voice. "It smells of seaweed!"

Chris spun round, trying to see who had spoken – but there was no one there. The only other people on the beach that day were an elderly couple who had gone on the same boat trip as his parents. Aside from Mikey and Ella, now making their way back from the rock pools, he was completely alone.

"Perhaps I'm going crazy from boredom!" Chris said to himself.

"Perhaps you are!" agreed the sharp voice.

This time, Chris jumped to his feet. The voice had seemed to come to him on the wind, as though it was surrounding him.

"What's the matter?" asked Ella as she and Mikey arrived back at their spot. The toddler dropped to his knees, grabbed his spade and turned his attention back to the hole he had been digging.

"I... I think we should go back to the cottage," said Chris.

"I thought it was *boring*," Ella reminded him.

"Boring, yes! Creepy – no!"

"Creepy?" said Ella. "What are you on about?"

"There was a voice," said Chris, with a shiver. "It... It agreed with me."

Ella picked up a baseball cap from the sand at her feet. "I think you've had too much sun," she said. "Mum told you to keep your hat on when you're out here."

Chris snatched the cap and tossed it away. "I don't need a hat!" he snapped.

"You do if you're imagining strange voices," said Ella.

"I didn't imagine it!" Chris insisted. "Someone spoke to me."

"Who?"

"I don't know!"

"It was the lady," said Mikey quietly.

"Yes!" hissed the sharp voice. "It *was* the lady!"

Chapter 2

The Curse

Slowly, Chris and Ella turned to look at where their young brother was digging. The sand he had excavated from his hole sat in a small mound beside him and there – carved into the mound – was the face of a haggard, old woman. She gazed up at the twins and her mouth split into a crooked smile.

"Boo!" she croaked. And then she began to rise up out of the ground.

Chris and Ella stepped back in terror as the sand shifted and grew. The shape

– just a lumpy column at first – began to twist and turn as first arms and then legs appeared. The figure cackled as she stretched out her hands, grains of sand falling away to reveal long, bent fingers tipped with broken nails.

Within minutes, the woman was taller than them, peering down at the children with sandy eyes. More and more grains fell away with every blink. Then, she reached down, plunging a fist into the sand and pulling out a pointed hat which she slapped onto her head.

"Who... Who are you?" gulped Ella.

The old hag grinned, revealing a handful of chipped, gritty teeth. "Me? I am The Sand Witch!" she croaked.

"A Sand Witch?" giggled Chris. "No thanks – I've already had my lunch!"

Ella elbowed him in the ribs. "Don't make fun of the monster made of sand!" she hissed.

"A monster, am I?" demanded the witch. "Yes, to the likes of you, I suppose I am. Cursed to spend eternity beneath the feet of holidaymakers – but not for much longer..."

"Much longer?" Chris asked.

The Sand Witch shuffled towards them a step. "Because – at long last – there are just innocent children alone on the beach. Innocent children with no grown-ups around to protect them!"

Ella glanced at her twin brother. She didn't like the sound of this. "We can protect ourselves!" she said.

"Maybe *you* can," spat the witch "but this little one can't!" And with that, she lunged out with a sandy arm and tried to grab Mikey.

"Leave him alone!" yelled Ella, holding tight to her little brother.

"Never!" barked the Sand Witch, flecks of sandy spittle flying from the end of her pointed tongue. "I can only pass on my curse to an innocent child – and *he* is about as innocent as they come."

"What do you mean?" asked Chris nervously.

The Sand Witch's yellow eyes flashed. "In just a few moment's time, I shall be free and your baby brother will be turned to sand in my place. He will remain part of this dratted beach for all eternity!"

Chapter 3

Washed Away

The Sand Witch reached out towards Mikey, her long, gnarled fingers quivering with excitement. "The little boy shall be mine!" she snarled. "He shall take my place and remain here forever as part of the beach, while I shall be free! FREE!" She threw her head back and cackled long and hard.

"Not if I've got anything to do with it!" cried Chris. He snatched up Mikey's plastic spade and ran at the witch, anger etched on his features. "Nobody threatens my little brother!" He lashed out with the spade, catching the Sand Witch in the shoulder. To his astonishment, the plastic spade sank deep into the sand beside her neck. Her sandy arm flopped down onto the beach with a FLUMPH!

Chris paused, the spade raised above his head.

"Why are you stopping?" Ella demanded.

Chris turned to look at her, his face pale. "I just chopped her arm off!" he said.

"It's not a *real* arm!" Ella reminded him.

Totally ignoring her injury, the Sand Witch laughed again. "Oh, this is going to be easier than I thought!" she spat.

She turned her gaze back to Mikey, reaching out with her remaining arm, "Come here, little boy!"

Ella grabbed Mikey's bucket and leapt forward. "Well, if you're not going to do it," she snapped at Chris, "I will!" She swung the bucket round in the air. It collided with the side of the witch's head and sand splattered across the beach.

"You're such a wimp, Chris!" Ella grunted, as she swung the bucket round again, this time sending the Sand Witch's hat flying. "She's made of sand! It's just like breaking up a sand sculpture!"

"But, I like sand sculptures!"

"Even sand sculptures that want to steal Mikey away from us?"

Chris glanced down at his baby brother, trembling behind Ella's legs, and his expression hardened. "No chance!" he growled. He gripped the spade and advanced on the Sand Witch. The old crone began to back away towards the sea, shrieking angrily.

"Leave my baby brother alone!" Chris warned.

"Never!" crowed the witch. "He's mine now! I just have to – aargh!"

Suddenly, a large wave swept in up the beach. The water enveloped the witch's feet and the columns of sand which made up her legs began to melt away. Chris and Ella watched as the witch collapsed into the waves, her cries echoing off the cliffs that bordered the beach.

"You haven't seen the last of me!" the crone croaked as she crumbled away, piece by piece, like a sandcastle when the tide comes in.

"Oh, yes we have!" roared Ella, jumping up and down on the only part of the witch that remained visible on the beach – her crooked pointy hat. Eventually, even that was gone and all was silent once more. The children slumped to the ground, exhausted. They pulled Mikey in towards them and gave him a hug. The sea continued to wash in and out below them.

"It's OK, buddy!" Chris said, wiping away his brother's tears. "She's gone now."

"Do you think she'll come back?" asked Ella.

Chris looked down at the waves. "Hopefully, the sea has washed her far away by now."

Ella checked her watch. "There's still an hour until Mum and Dad get back from their boat trip," she said. "I think we'd better get back up to the cottage and stay inside until they return – unless you still think it's boring up there, of course...."

Chris shivered. "No, it's OK," he said as bravely as he could. "I'll come back to the cottage with you two – you know, just to make sure you're both safe." He jumped to his feet and struck a dramatic martial arts pose. "You might need me to save you both again."

"My hero," said Ella flatly. "Now, come on – let's get this lot packed up."

Working as quickly as they could, the twins gathered together the things they'd brought down to the beach that morning: their baseball caps, Mikey's bucket and spade, the beach ball, Chris's flippers and scuba mask, Ella's book, and the bottle of sunscreen. By the time they had everything, their arms were piled high.

"Let's go," said Ella, tucking her book under her chin so she could hold Mikey's hand. She had taken a few steps up the path towards the cottage when she realized that Chris wasn't with them. She turned to find her twin brother still standing on the sand.

"I said, come on!" she called. "The sooner we get back to the cottage, the better."

"I can't!" hissed Chris through gritted teeth.

"What do you mean you can't?" said Ella. "You're not carrying that much stuff. I've got more than you, *and* I'm holding Mikey's hand."

"I don't mean that," said Chris. "I mean, I can't move. Something's got hold of my ankle!"

Chapter 4

Run!

Ella looked down at Chris's feet and jumped with fright. A hand was sticking up out of the sand, and it had a tight grip around her brother's leg. A hand with twisted fingers and long broken nails – all made out of sand.

"Don't move!" she said as quietly as she could.

"I *can't* move!" Chris reminded her. "Is it her?"

Ella nodded. She tossed her armful of stuff aside and ran back along the path, diving into the sand and tearing at the hand gripping Chris's ankle. But, as soon as she released him from the witch's grip – another hand appeared to grab his other foot. Ella punched that hand away with her fist – only for the first hand to return.

"I can't get you free!" she shouted to Chris.

But, suddenly, the witch's hands released Chris's legs of their own accord, and they began to push through the sand, dragging themselves away, bony elbows rising and falling as they moved. It looked as though the witch was swimming away from them through the sand! And she was swimming in Mikey's direction.

The toddler stood at the foot of the path, his eyes wide with horror as the witch swam closer and closer. The tip of her pointed hat rose from beneath the beach, looking for all the world like the fin of an approaching shark.

"Run, Mikey! Run!" shouted Ella.

The toddler didn't need telling twice. He turned and raced as fast as he could towards the cottage door. Behind him, the witch was swimming faster now, her pointed nose and deformed face rising up above the sand.

The twins gave chase. "If we're lucky, she won't be able to leave the beach itself!" yelled Ella. But, as she spoke, the Sand Witch leapt out of the ground and landed lightly on the grey stone of the cottage path. She paused only to flash a twisted smile to the twins, then she ran after Mikey, laughing wickedly.

"I guess we're not lucky, then!" cried Chris, putting on an extra burst of speed. But he and Ella were too far back. They wouldn't be able to catch the witch before she got to their little brother.

Mikey reached the door of the cottage and pushed it open, looking back for the twins.

"Get inside!" Ella shouted. "And lock the door!"

Mikey dashed inside and slammed the door with a BANG – just as the witch reached the doorstep.

CLICK!

Mikey appeared at one of the cottage windows, peering out. He had the key in his hand.

Chris and Ella skidded to halt behind the witch. "Well," said Chris with a smile. "What are you going to do now?"

Snarling, the Sand Witch raised a finger and held it out towards the keyhole on the door.

"You can't unlock it from out here," said Ella. "There's only one key, and Mikey's got it."

"Who says I mean to unlock it?" asked the witch – then she pushed her finger deep into the keyhole. There was a faint HISS as grains of sand began to flow through the tiny hole and gather on the floor at the other side of the door.

"She's pouring herself through the lock!" cried Ella. "She's pouring herself inside the cottage with Mikey!"

The twins set off at a run but, before they could get any closer, the

Sand Witch thrust out her other hand towards them. Gripped in her fingers was an old piece of driftwood.

Chris swallowed hard. "Tell me that's not a magic wand!" he whispered.

Chapter 5

Claws of Doom!

Ella didn't have time to reply. A flash of sand–coloured light erupted from the end of the Sand Witch's wand. Then she cackled, turning her attention back to the door and continuing to pour herself, grain by grain, through the keyhole.

Inside the cottage, Mikey hammered on the window and called out to his brother and sister. But the twins suddenly found that they couldn't move.

"I feel weird!" said Chris. "My whole body is tingling!"

"I've got the same feeling," said Ella.

"Do you think she's cast some sort of spell on us?" asked Chris.

"Probably," Ella replied. "But, I can't imagine the Sand Witch just wants to give us pins and needles."

Suddenly, Chris gasped. "I don't think she cast a spell on *us*!" he exclaimed. "Look! Everything's getting bigger – the cottage, the cliffs… the whole beach!"

"It's not the beach that's getting bigger, Chris!" said Ella with a gulp. "*We're* getting smaller!"

Chris stared down at himself in horror. It was true! He and Ella were shrinking! "This isn't fair!" he moaned. "I'm already one of the shortest kids in our class. Now I won't even be able to climb on to my chair!"

The twins were now half their original size.

"Please let this end soon!" cried Ella.

"Your voice has gone all squeaky!" said Chris. Then he clamped a hand over his mouth. "So has mine! I sound like a cartoon hamster!"

The twins shrank smaller and smaller, until they were the same height as Mikey's yellow plastic bucket. Ella slumped back against the now-massive bottle of sunscreen in an attempt to ease her dizziness. "I think that's it," she breathed. "This is as small as we're going to get."

"So, what do we do now?" Chris croaked.

"The same as we were doing before," Ella insisted. "We get to the cottage and save Mikey."

Chris jumped up onto his scuba mask and peered up the path to the holiday home. What had only been four or five metres a few seconds ago now looked like a hike of several miles.

"It'll take us ages to reach the cottage now!" he moaned.

"Well, we have to think of something, and fast!" said Ella. "The Sand Witch is over halfway inside the cottage!"

"If only we had some kind of transport…" said Chris.

CLICK! CLICK! CLICK!

Chris turned to stare at his sister. "What did you say that for?"

Ella's brow furrowed. "I didn't say anything."

"Yes, you did!" Chris insisted. "You clicked at me."

"No, I didn't!"

CLICK! CLICK! CLICK!"

"There! You did it again!"

"That wasn't me!" said Ella.

"Then who was it?"

CLICK! CLICK! CLICK!

Slowly, Chris and Ella turned to see a crab scuttling towards them, its pincers clicking. But this crab was the size of a car!

"It's a huge mutant!" yelled Chris.

"No, it's not!" Ella reminded him. "It's the tiny crab Mikey and I took back to the rock pool earlier. We're the same size as it now."

The crab edged closer. The creature's lipless mouth opened and closed as it drooled at the sight of a potential meal.

"It doesn't seem to be too pleased that you dumped it in a rock pool!" Chris pointed out. "What do we do?"

Ella snatched Chris's snorkel from beside the swimming mask and twirled it like a martial arts weapon. "We fight!" she growled.

The crab lunged forward, the larger of its two claws snapping dangerously close to Ella's face. Ella spun the snorkel and brought it down on the crab's shell with a thud. The animal clicked with rage and retreated a few paces before attacking once again.

Chris dived beneath one of his discarded flippers and watched from between his fingers as his sister matched the vast crustacean blow for blow. The crab snapped left – Ella blocked its assault on the right with the snorkel. The crab darted to its right and Ella flipped its sharp pincer away with a kick to the left.

Frustrated, the crab crouched down on its legs, then leapt through the air at Ella, claws cracking together like claps of thunder. Ella dropped flat, causing the crab to sail over her. It crashed to the ground at the foot of the path. Quick as a flash, Ella jumped up and tipped Mikey's bucket over, trapping the angry crab underneath.

"Right!" she said, tossing the snorkel aside and helping Chris out from under the flipper. "Let's get up to the cottage and save Mikey!"

Chapter 6

Flight into Danger

"We still need a way to get there," said Chris. "And I've had an idea…" Dragging the flipper aside, he revealed a large rectangle wrapped in silver tin foil.

"What's that?" asked Ella

Chris began to unwrap the foil. "It's what's left of our lunch," he said as he pulled at the metallic material. He looked as though he was peeling back the duvet from a double bed. "Mikey left the crusts of his sandwiches – as usual – and I reckon we can use them to get to the cottage." With that, he grabbed a huge hunk of bread and held it up above his head.

"Be careful," Ella warned. "You might attract–"

Before she could finish, there was a screech from above. The twins gazed up into the clear blue sky to see the silhouette of a seagull swooping down towards them. Its growing shadow enveloped the twins.

"Chris!" Ella yelled. "Put the bread away now!"

"Not just yet," said Chris. "Get ready to jump in one… two… three!"

As the seagull dived for the piece of bread, Chris quickly dumped the treat and jumped, gripping onto the flying bird's leg.

"I hope you know what you're doing!" yelled Ella as she leapt into the air and grabbed the seagull's other leg.

"Of course I know what I'm doing!" Chris shouted back. "I'm getting us to the cottage door!" The twins looked ahead. The only part of the witch left to trickle through the keyhole now was her legs. They could see Mikey in the cottage's living room, his fists banging on the window as they flew closer, dangling beneath the soaring seabird.

Suddenly, a draft of air caught beneath the gull's wings and it veered to the left. "We're going to miss the cottage!" cried Ella.

"Not if I can help it!" shouted Chris. He released the bird's leg with one hand

and reached up to pluck a feather out of the gull's underbelly.

CAW! The seagull twisted in the air and resumed its course towards the cottage door. "OK!" bellowed Chris as they neared their destination. "When I say three – let go of the seagull and drop down into the flower bed next to the path!"

Ella opened her mouth to reply but before she could speak, Chris roared "Three!" The twins let go of the seagull and fell through the air, crashing down onto the soil of the cottage's well-maintained garden.

"Ow!" moaned Chris, sitting up and rubbing his back. "That really hurt!"

Ella pulled a huge rose thorn from her thigh and glared at him. "Then why did you tell us to do it?!"

"Because it's our only way of saving Mikey!" Chris replied. He pointed to the cottage door. "Look!"

Ella gasped. The final few grains of sand that made up the Sand Witch had disappeared. The hag was now inside the cottage with their baby brother! The twins jumped up and ran to the door.

"How do we get inside?" asked Chris, peering up at the door handle far, far above them.

"Not by going up there," said Ella, lying flat on her stomach. "We'll have to wiggle under here." She began to shuffle forward, squeezing herself under the front door of their holiday cottage.

"Well," said Chris to himself. "If you can't beat them – join them!" And with that, he too began to wriggle through the gap.

The twins emerged on the other side to hear a pounding THUMP! THUMP! THUMP! THUMP! At first, Chris thought there was an earthquake, and that the holiday cottage was about to collapse around them. But then he looked up to see his baby brother – Mikey – walking backwards in their direction.

"He's a lot bigger than I remember him!" Chris remarked.

The toddler was backing away from the Sand Witch. The old crone was advancing on Mikey – a long, gnarled finger pointed directly at him. "You shall take my place and be part of this beach forever!" she cackled as she advanced.

"Not while we're here!" squeaked Ella. She grabbed Chris's hand and ran in front of Mikey. The twins held up their hands in an effort to stop the witch, even though they barely reached higher than her sandy ankles.

"You cannot stop me!" sneered the Sand Witch, aiming her driftwood wand down at the tiny twins. "Obviously shrinking you wasn't enough! Let's see how you like being zapped into little bits…"

"NO!" cried Mikey. "Leave them alone!" The toddler leapt over his tiny brother and sister and snatched the wand from the witch.

"Give that back!" the old woman screeched. "You don't know how powerful it is!"

But Mikey just shook his head. Then, with a determined expression on his face, he waved the magic wand in the air....

Chapter 7

The Cave Below

The floorboards in front of the children began to crack and splinter. The tiny twins were forced to jump back to avoid being speared by one of the sharp shards of wood that shot up from the ground.

"You fools!" screeched the Sand Witch, staring at the fracture in the floor. "You don't know what you've done!"

The crack grew quickly, stretching from one side of the room to the other in a matter of seconds. There was a creak – like the sound of a huge tree twisting and bending in a strong wind – and then the floor began to split apart, revealing a deep, dark chasm below.

"What's going on?" squeaked Ella.

"I don't know!" croaked Chris. "But mum and dad are not going to be happy about this!"

There was a crash as a portion of the floor in front of the children fell away into the rapidly expanding hole. Ella turned and launched herself at the nearest piece of furniture – the sofa. She grabbed on to the patterned material dangling from the base of the couch just as the ground vanished beneath her feet. For a second, she swung helplessly, her knuckles white as she clung onto the bottom of the sofa – then a huge hand reached down and plucked her to safety.

Mikey gently cupped his sister in his palm and lifted her on to the sofa cushions where she found Chris struggling to catch his breath. "Mikey saved me!" she exclaimed, smiling up at her younger brother.

"Me too," said Chris. "It really pays off having a giant toddler in the family!"

"Well I definitely prefer being bigger than my little brother," Ella replied. "But we won't grow again unless that Sand Witch reverses her shrinking spell. Where is she? I'm really starting to lose my temper with her!"

The twins crawled to the edge of the sofa cushion and stared across the room. The Sand Witch was pressed against the far wall, standing on a thin strip of wood – all that was left of her side of the cottage floor. Between them, the vast hole spread out like a miniaturized version of the Grand Canyon, steep piles of rocks on either side leading down into the dark.

Rivulets of sand began to run down the Sand Witch's face. Her hat was collapsing in on itself. "Give me back my wand this instant!" she bellowed, flattening herself against the wall.

Mikey glanced at the piece of driftwood in his hand, then he hid it behind his back. "NO!" he shouted.

The witch snarled, fixing her gaze on Chris and Ella. "Tell your stubborn baby brother to return my wand at once!" she hissed. "I can't survive without it! I'll disintegrate!"

"Will you turn us back to our proper size if he does?" demanded Chris.

"Yes – of course!" spat the witch.

"And forget about passing your curse on to Mikey?" added Ella. "You have to go away and leave us all alone!"

The length of wood beneath the Sand Witch creaked and shifted slightly. "Yes!" she screeched as the brim of her hat dropped off with a SPLUPH. "Anything you want! Just hurry up!"

"OK," said Ella. She turned and looked up at her younger brother, towering above them. "Mikey – give the wand back to the witch."

"No!" said the toddler. "She's naughty!"

"Yes, she is naughty," said Ella. "But she's very sorry now, and she wants to put everything back to normal."

Mikey brought the wand out from behind his back. "Does she promise?"

Ella looked across the room to the witch. "Well?"

"Well, what?"

"Do you promise to be good and fix everything once you have your wand back?"

The Sand Witch's face twisted into an expression of discomfort. "Yes," she snarled, as though the very words were painful to say. "I promise to be good and fix everything. Now, give me back my wand!"

Mikey sighed, then held out his hand. The wand barely reached out over the hole in the floor.

"How am I supposed to reach that?" snapped the witch. Her shoulders began to dribble away, grain by grain.

"It's your wand," said Chris. "You find a way!"

"You're the ones who want to be back to their normal size," the Sand Witch countered. "So, *you* find a way...."

"I could sit on it and fly across," Chris suggested. "It might work like a witch's broomstick."

"You've been reading too many fairy tales, boy!" the witch snarled. "Broomsticks don't fly in real life – and neither do wands!"

"You could trickle your way over to this side of the room," said Ella.

The witch risked a glance down at the dark abyss between them. "I'm not moving an inch!" she hissed.

"Then there's only one thing for it," said Chris. "Mikey – you'll have to throw the wand across to the witch, and she'll have to catch it."

"OK, said Mikey, swinging his arm back.

"Wait!" yelled the witch, "be careful it doesn't...."

But it was too late. Mikey had already hurled the piece of driftwood with all his might. Everyone watched as it soared through the air, spinning end to end – almost in slow motion. The witch raised a hand, sandy fingers spread ready to catch it....

...and then the end of the wand clipped the glass lightshade hanging from the ceiling. Instantly, it began to fall – straight into the shadowy pit that had once been the cottage floor.

"You stupid child!" screamed the Sand Witch.

Mikey's bottom lip began to tremble and his eyes filled with tears. "It's not his fault!" snapped Ella. "He's only three!" She reached up and took her brother's thumb in her hand.

"Oh, boo hoo!" jeered the witch. "I don't care how old he is. Now he's lost my wand, I'll never be able to rid myself of this blasted curse!"

"Don't you mean return us to our normal size and fix the floor?" asked Chris.

"It doesn't matter what I mean!" the old woman barked. "The wand has gone – into exactly the same cave where my spell book vanished all those years ago."

"Your spell book?" asked Ella.

The witch nodded. Her hat had now completely wasted away and her sandy hair was starting to fall out in clumps. "My sister and I used to live in this house. We fell out over the ingredients for a new spell, and she cursed me to be made of sand and remain part of this beach for all eternity."

"Wow," said Chris, glancing at his sister. "And I thought our fights were bad!"

"Before she left," the witch continued. "She opened up the ground and placed my spell book in the deepest cave she could find, ensuring I could never reverse her magic and return to life."

"But you're made of sand!" said Ella. "Couldn't you trickle down there and get it back?"

The old woman shook her head. "I tried many times," she said sadly. "But she'd hidden the book in a tiny crack in the rock. Every time I reached in to get it, there wasn't enough room to reform my hand and pull it out. It's lost forever."

"Unless you had some tiny people to drop down inside that tiny crack," Chris suggested.

Ella stared at her brother in surprise. "What do you mean?"

"*We're* tiny!" said Chris. "We could get into a thin crack and get the book back. It could be our only chance to put everything right."

Ella peered over the edge of the sofa into the yawning chasm. "But how do we get down there?"

"That," said Chris, "would be down to Mikey. He looked up at his younger brother. "Fancy a climb, buddy?"

"Yes!" Mikey beamed. He snatched up the twins and tucked them into the chest pocket of his dungarees, then he carefully stepped over the edge of the wooden floor and on to the first rock below.

Chapter 8

Into the Depths

"Hurry!" cried the witch. Ella glanced up at her. Her hair had almost disappeared now, and patches of her scalp were crumbling away.

"Be careful!" cried Ella as Mikey climbed deeper and deeper into the darkness.

"He'll be fine," Chris reassured her. "The climbing frame at the park is much steeper than this, and he plays on that all the time."

Slowly, Mikey climbed lower and lower, carefully finding handholds and making sure his trainers didn't slip on the jagged stones before trusting his weight to them. The descent took around 20 minutes but, eventually, they reached the bottom of the pit.

Chris glanced up. "Look at that!" he said. Ella and Mikey followed his gaze. High above them was the fractured hole in the cottage floor. It looked like a yawning mouth with broken, snapping teeth. Thankfully, the ceiling light bulb hadn't broken when the wand had hit its shade and it provided a dim glow by which the children could search the bottom of the cavern.

Mikey lifted the twins from his pocket and placed them onto the ground. Glistening, dark grey walls of rough stones surrounded them on all sides.

Water trickled down the rocks, the droplets plopping noisily into a pile of sand beside them. Chris began to climb up over the mound to get a better view of his surroundings, then froze.

"Yuk!" he said.

"What's the matter?" asked Ella.

Chris shook some of the wet sand from his shoe. "I think this is made up of the bits of the witch that have melted away! I'm climbing over her!"

As he spoke, another shower of sand dropped onto his head. "Aargh!" he yelled as he jumped from the mound, brushing the grains from his hair.

"Here's the wand!" said Ella, running over to the piece of driftwood. Mikey grabbed the stick and tucked it into his waistband.

"And here's the book!" cried Chris from the other side of the cave. "The Sand Witch is right, though – it's stuck in a small crevice."

The grains of sand were falling around them like rain now and, above, they could hear the witch shrieking with terror.

"Will you be able to get inside?" asked Ella.

"No problem!" grinned Chris. And, with that, he began to wriggle into the tiny gap beside the book. He could feel the rough leather cover rubbing against his cheek as he squeezed past it. After a moment, he reached the bottom of the crack. "I'm going to push it up from here!" he called out. "See if you can pull it out!"

"Ready when you are!" shouted Ella.

Forcing his tiny hands underneath the book, Chris began to heave it upwards out of the crack in the rock.

Slowly, the book began to move – inch by inch. Ella and Mikey grabbed the edges of the cover from the other end and pulled as hard as they could. Then the book slid out of its cramped prison and landed with a crash on the ground.

After a second, Chris appeared from the crevice, brushing dirt from his t-shirt.

"We did it!" beamed Ella, hugging her brother. "Now, let's get back up to the cottage."

"Please help me!" screeched the Sand Witch far above them. "There isn't much of me left!"

"Hang on a second," said Chris. He ran around to the other side of the book and flipped open the cover. "This is a book of spells, right? And we've also got the witch's magic wand."

Ella frowned. "So?"

"So, we don't know if we can trust the Sand Witch enough to hand them back to her. Less than an hour ago, she was trying to turn Mikey into a bit of the beach!"

The huge toddler nodded. "She's a naughty lady."

"But she only did that because she's sad," said Ella. "She said her sister hid the spell book to stop her reversing her curse."

"You're suggesting we help her?" said Chris.

"I don't know," Ella admitted.

Chris sighed. "Well, before we go any further, we've got a decision to make...."

Chapter 9

A Spell of Trouble

The Sand Witch screamed as her entire head collapsed in on itself, thick plumes of sand tumbling down into the cavern below. Ella grabbed Chris's arm and pulled him clear of the cascade.

"Well?" she asked. "What do we do? Help the witch, or fix this ourselves?"

Chris glanced up at what remained of the witch as she fell apart above them. "I don't think she was *really* going to help us," he said firmly. "So we don't help her."

Ella raced over to the spell book and began leafing through it. This wasn't an easy task now that the pages were bigger than her. "Then we have to find the spell that will make us grow back to our normal size," she said. Chris joined her at the book and, together, they began to search. "Don't lose that magic wand, Mikey!" he said to their younger brother.

"Got it!" beamed Mikey, gripping the length of driftwood tightly in his fist.

Ella read the names of the spells out as she and Chris studied the witch's book of magic. "*Turn your victim into a tree... Gain the ability to talk to foxes... Cure very pointy elbows... Shrink your enemy down to size...* We don't want that one again!"

There was a WUMPH! behind them. Chris jumped. "What was that?"

Ella took a step back and stared up through the hole in the cottage floor above them. "I think it was the Sand Witch's body. There's not much left of her now."

"There won't be much left of us if Mum and Dad come home before we can fix this lot," said Chris, flicking through more of the spell book's pages. "All we had to do was look after Mikey while they went on a boat trip – now we've wrecked the cottage and we're ten times smaller than our baby brother!"

"Maybe we should have asked the Sand Witch for help after all," said Ella. There was a HISS as the final part of the old woman rained down around them.

"Bit late for that now," said Chris, brushing the sand from his hair. "It's not like we can go back in time."

"Maybe we can't reverse time," said Ella with a smile. "But we could reverse a spell..."

Chris looked confused. "What?"

Ella flicked back through the pages of the book until she reached the shrinking spell. "This must be the spell the witch used to miniaturize us," she said. "So, what would happen if we said the spell backwards?"

"Do you think that would work?" asked Chris. "You think we might grow again?"

Ella shrugged. "It's worth a try..."

"Go on then," said Chris. "It can't get any worse than this."

"Right," said Ella, studying the words. "The spell says Small, Smaller, Smallest!", so I'm going to read that out backwards. Mikey – wave the magic wand... NOW!"

The toddler swung the piece of driftwood back and forth over the tiny twins' heads as Ella chanted the spell in reverse...

"Tsellams, Rellams, Llams!"

A sand coloured light flooded the cavern, and Mikey found himself tingling. "Something's happening!" he cried. He screwed his eyes tight and crossed his fingers.

Suddenly, there was a bright FLASH! and Chris felt something hard crack against his head. "Ow!" he moaned, opening his eyes and rubbing at the sore spot. Then he grinned. He had bumped his head on a rock jutting out from halfway up the cave wall. "We're big again!"

"Yes, we are," said Ella. "But that's not all..."

Chris turned to look at his sister. "What do you mea–" The words stuck in his throat. Standing in front of him was another Chris! They were both back to their normal sizes, but Ella had changed into a boy that looked just like him!

"This isn't good," she said.

"Of course it's good!" exclaimed Chris. "In fact, it's perfect! I've got a twin brother!"

"I used to have one of those," said Ella.

Chris flicked his long, blonde hair out of his eyes. "I don't understand," he said. Then he froze, and pulled the hair back in front of his face. "Why's my hair so long?"

"It's not just your hair..." Ella pointed out.

Slowly Chris looked down at himself. "I'm a girl!" he yelled.

"And I'm a boy!" said Ella.

"Yes, but... I'm a *girl*!"

Mikey giggled. "You're funny!"

"I'm not funny!" barked Chris. "I'm a *girl*!"

"I think the spell went wrong," said Ella.

"Of course it went wrong! I'm a *girl*!"

"Stop saying that!"

"But, it's true! I'm a *girl*!"

"And just repeating it isn't going to help us," Ella pointed out. "We must have switched bodies somehow." She picked up the book and began to read. "Now we just have to find the right bit of magic to swap us back."

"No way!" said Chris, snatching the spell book from Ella's hands. "We're not messing with any more of this stuff. I might end up with two heads, or twelve feet, or – worst of all – stuck as a *girl* forever!"

"I'm not exactly happy about being a boy, either!" said Ella.

"Then we need help!" cried Chris. He dropped to his knees and began to scoop up handfuls of sand from the cavern floor. "Sand Witch!" he called. "Are you in there?"

"Mm-humph-mmm," said a voice.

"What was that?" asked Chris.

"Mm-humph-mmm-humph-mmm!" said the voice.

"It's the Sand Witch," said Ella. "She hasn't got a mouth to speak with."

Chris leapt towards the pile of sand and quickly fashioned a nose, a mouth and a pair of eyes in the middle of it.

"What do you want?" the mouth muttered.

"We need you to turn me back into a boy!" said Chris.

"And me back to a girl," Ella reminded him.

"Yeah, that too."

The pile of sand sighed. "Just leave me alone."

"But we can help you!" said Chris. "We'll help you get rid of your curse!"

The two sharp eyes flicked across to Mikey. "You're going to give me the child?"

Chris paused as he thought for a moment.

Ella slapped his shoulder. "Of course we're not!" she said.

"Of course we're not!" repeated Chris. Then he smiled as an idea occurred. "Do you have to pass the curse on to another human?"

"That's an interesting question," the mouth replied, eyes narrowing. Then the pile of sand shook itself. "No, I suppose not."

"Then I know just what to do!" Chris jumped to his feet.

"Where are you going?" asked Ella.

Chris grinned. "To settle a score!" Then he reached up and grabbed the rocks above his head and began to climb.

Chapter 10

Claws for Thought

It wasn't easy – climbing in a dress – but eventually, Chris pulled himself out of the hole and sat on what was left of the cottage floor. Moving carefully, he inched his way along the remaining floorboard to the door, and then dashed out into the sunshine.

He raced down the path to the edge of the beach where he and Ella had abandoned their belongings earlier. He stepped over his snorkel and flippers to carefully lift up Mikey's yellow bucket.

There, pacing about beneath it, and looking furious, was the tiny crab.

"You're coming with me!" said Chris. Using the plastic spade, he lifted the crab and dropped it into the bucket, then he turned to head back to the cottage.

"Ella!" called a voice. "Ella!" It was a moment before Chris realized that he looked like his sister and that someone was calling him.

He turned towards the voice, and his heart sank. A boat had pulled up among the waves – and his parents were walking up the beach towards him!

"Oh, er... Hi, Mum! Hi, Dad!" he cried, trying to sound like a girl. "You're back!" He swung the bucket behind himself. "How was the boat trip?"

"It was lovely!" his mum shouted. "How have you lot been? Have the boys given you any trouble?"

"Not exactly..." said Chris. "I'll, er... let them know you're coming!" He turned and ran as fast as he could back up to the cottage.

"Mum and Dad are here!" he shouted as he skidded to a halt beside the edge of the hole.

"No!" cried Ella from the depths of the cavern.

"Yes! Now, catch!" Chris tipped the bucket over, dropping the crab down into the hole. Ella reached out and caught it.

"Ow!" she yelped as the crab nipped her.

"That little fellow will do perfectly!" the mouth cackled. "I don't know why I didn't think of it years ago!"

"Quickly!" cried Ella, holding the crab carefully between her fingers.

"Right, tap the wand against the wall in a steady rhythm, tap, tap, tap," ordered the Sand Witch.

Mikey did as he was told, and the witch began to mutter under her breath.

CRASH! Suddenly the whole house began to spin around...

* * *

Mum and Dad pushed open the door to the cottage and stared. "What's going on here?' asked Dad.

Chris found himself sitting on the polished wooden floorboards of the living room. The hole was gone, and there was no sign of the witch. He reached up and ran his fingers through his hair – which was thankfully very short. He was a boy again!

"What do you mean?" he asked.

I mean *that*!" said Dad, pointing to a tiny… sandy… something running from side to side in front of Mikey. "What is it?"

"Oh it's just a crab," said Ella, scooping it up. "Mikey found it on the beach."

Mum shook her head. "I know it's exciting seeing different creatures here at the seaside," she said. "But you shouldn't bring them inside the cottage."

"Sorry," said Chris, holding out the bucket as Ella dropped the crab inside. "We'll just take it back to the beach."

"Good idea," said Dad. "Then we'll have some lunch. Come on Mikey!"

As their parents and little brother disappeared into the kitchen, Chris and Ella hurried outside. At the bottom of the path, they released the surprised creature back onto the sand. It clicked its pincers excitedly, then sank beneath the surface, grain by grain.

Ella sighed. "We did it!" she beamed. "And I don't know about you, but I'm hungry."

"Me, too!" said Chris, reaching for his snorkel and mask – but they weren't there. "My flippers have gone missing, as well!" he cried.

"I think I know where they are," said Ella, pointing down the beach to the sea. Chris shielded his eyes against the bright summer sun and followed her gaze. There, skipping happily into the waves, was an old woman with greenish skin. She was wearing snorkelling gear and cackling to herself.

The twins sat down on the sand and watched as the woman lowered herself into the water, the tip of her pointed hat sinking slowly down until it was gone from sight.

"Still think the beach is boring?" asked Ella.

"Definitely not!" replied Chris.

"Hey, you two!" shouted a voice. Chris and Ella turned. Their Dad was standing in the doorway to the cottage. "Come inside – there's a sandwich waiting for you!"

THE END

FICTION EXPRESS

THE READERS TAKE CONTROL!

Have you ever wanted to change the course of a plot, change a character's destiny, tell an author what to write next?

Well, now you can!

'The Sand Witch' was originally written for the award-winning interactive e-book website Fiction Express.

Fiction Express e-books are published in gripping weekly episodes. At the end of each episode, readers are given voting options to decide where the plot goes next. They vote online and the winning vote is then conveyed to the author who writes the next episode, in real time, according to the readers' most popular choice.

www.fictionexpress.co.uk

WINNER
Education Resources
Award for Innovation

FICTION EXPRESS

TALK TO THE AUTHORS

The Fiction Express website features a blog where readers can interact with the authors while they are writing. An exciting and unique opportunity!

FANTASTIC TEACHER RESOURCES

Each weekly Fiction Express episode comes with a PDF of teacher resources packed with ideas to extend the text.

"The teaching resources are fab and easily fill a whole week of literacy lessons!"
Rachel Humphries, teacher at Westacre Middle School

If you enjoyed this story, you might also
like to read *Rise of the Rabbits.*
Here is a taster for you…

Chapter 1

Rabbit on the Loose

The day the school rabbit tried to kill
everyone started out pretty much like
any other.

I woke up early, like I always do.
My twin brother, Harvey, finally
dragged himself out of bed at half past
eight as usual. Mum says if sleeping
ever became an Olympic sport, Harvey
and my dad would compete for gold
every time.

Mind you, at least Dad does something useful when he's awake. He's a botanist, which means he travels the world finding and collecting rare plants.

Harvey, on the other hand, doesn't do anything for anybody. He's either up in his room playing Minecraft or downstairs watching Minecraft videos on the laptop. Or he's finding new ways to be as annoying as humanly possible. Usually to me.

And then there's my mum. My mum is... well, she's kind of Supermum. I get up at 7 am every day, but Mum has already been up, taken our dog, Scraps, for a walk and started breakfast in that time.

Anyway, I should introduce myself. I'm Lola. I love swimming, archery and football, hate Minecraft (seriously, what's the point?), and when I'm older want to be either a top athlete, the prime minister… or maybe to win *The X-Factor*.

I *did* want to be a vet, but that was before what happened with the school rabbit, Mr Lugs…. But I'm getting ahead of myself.

Like I said, it all started normally enough. Harvey and I went to school (I like it, he hates it), had lunch in the canteen (I hate it, he loves it), then were picked to take Mr Lugs home for the weekend (we both liked that).

Dad was asleep on the armchair in the living room when we got home. He'd arrived back from a trip to some jungle or other the day before, so he kept nodding off because of the jetlag. Well, that was his excuse, anyway.

Harvey thought it would be funny to put Mr Lugs on Dad's lap while he was asleep, to see what would happen when he woke up. For once, I agreed with him, so I gently set the rabbit down on my dad's outstretched legs, then tiptoed away.

"This is going to be brilliant!" Harvey whispered. He took out his mobile phone and started recording. We half-crouched behind the couch and waited.

And waited.

And waited.

"Dad's a really deep sleeper, isn't he?" I said.

Mr Lugs was wriggling about on Dad's lap, his little nose twitching away like it always does. He's quite heavy for a rabbit, because the kids in school are always feeding him treats, but Dad still didn't notice.

"This is taking ages," Harvey grumbled. He cupped a hand to the side of his mouth and shouted, "DAD!"

Dad jolted awake. He looked down, saw Mr Lugs, then let out an ear-splitting scream. In one swift movement he leaped out of the seat, catapulting Mr Lugs across the room.

End over end the poor bunny flipped, twirling and spinning, his fluffy white fur making him look like a tiny cloud.

Jumping up from behind the couch I dived, arms reaching like a goalkeeper. Everything seemed to go into slow motion as I sailed through the air, hands together, fingers outstretched.

I saw Harvey turn his phone camera towards me. I heard Dad give a little gasp of shock. And I saw the look of pure terror on Mr Lugs's little face as he rocketed helplessly across the room.

I'm not going to make it, I thought, but then my fingertips felt something furry and my hands wrapped firmly around the tumbling bunny's body.

I landed with a *thud* on the carpet, almost winding myself. But it didn't matter. I had done it! I had saved Mr Lugs! Mr Lugs looked at me, and I'm pretty sure he smiled. Well, maybe not smiled, but he definitely blinked.

"Whoa," said Harvey, tapping the

screen of his phone, "that's *totally* going on YouTube!"

Dad was pretty impressed with the catch, but not so impressed by us putting a rabbit on him when he was asleep. He started going on about how the school shouldn't have sent Mr Lugs home with us, and about how it'd wind up the dog, and blah-de-blah-de-blah.

Luckily he sat down mid-rant, and almost immediately fell back to sleep. Mum was out walking Scraps, so Harvey and I decided we'd take it in turns to look after Mr Lugs. I wanted to go first, but Harvey insisted he do it.

FICTI⬤N EXPRESS

The Rise of the Rabbits
by Barry Hutchison

When twins Harvey and Lola are given the school rabbit, Mr Lugs, to look after for the weekend, they're both very excited. That is until the rabbit begins to mutate and decides the time has come for bunnies to rise up and seize control.

It's up to Harvey and Lola to find a way to return Mr Lugs and his friends to normal, before the menaces sweep across the country – and then the world!

ISBN 978-1-78322-540-8

FICTI⬤N EXPRESS

Snaffles the Cat Burglar
by Cavan Scott

When notorious feline felon Snaffles and his dim canine sidekick Bonehead are caught red-pawed trying to steal the Sensational Salmon of Sumatra, not everything is what it seems. Their capture leads them on a top-secret mission for the Ministry of Secret Shenanigans.

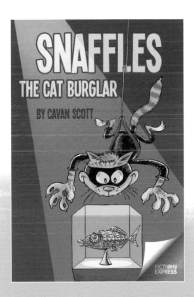

ISBN 978-1-78322-543-9

About the Author

Tommy Donbavand is the author of the popular 13-book Scream Street series for 7 to 10 year olds. His other books include *Zombie!*, *Wolf* and *Uniform* (winner of the Hackney Short Novel Award).

In theatre, Tommy's plays have been performed to thousands of children on national tours. These productions include *Hey Diddle Diddle*, *Rumplestiltskin*, *Jack & Jill In The Forgotten Nursery*, and *Humpty Dumpty And The Incredibly Daring Rescue Of The Alien Princess From Deep Space*. He is also responsible for five episodes of the CBBC TV series, *Planet Cook* (Platinum Films).